MW01243131

ANTON'S BOOK

A JOURNEY

ERIC GARVANNE, JR.

ISBN 987-1-0918-4036-2

Contact Information:
garvannethewriter@gmail.com
@diplomaticeric (Instagram/Twitter)

For Anton,

my nephew, my s.s.

"You then, my son, be strong in the grace that is in Christ Jesus. And the things you have heard me say in the presence of many witnesses entrust to reliable men who will also be qualified to teach others."

~2 Timothy 2:1-2

Table of Contents

INTRODUCTION

I originally wrote this book solely for the purpose of giving it to my teenage nephew Anton in 2018. I wanted to share—in a creative way—a part of my life that I knew would resonate with him.

For most of my life I struggled with feeling as though I didn't fit-in. I felt like a square peg trying to find its place in a world full of round holes. For many years, I privately hid the internal pain of the loneliness, depression, despair, confusion, awkwardness, rejection and unacceptance that seemed to follow me everywhere, no matter how hard I'd fight to overcome it.

Often, I sought to find an escape—to go to sleep and never wake up, or to simply kill myself. I thought suicide would be the only way to finally find lasting relief. However, publicly I smiled, laughed, counseled, worked, made the grades, encouraged others, and put on a front like everything was "okay" with me. I learned how to keep people from "reading" me and getting too close to my heart, so they wouldn't know what I was truly thinking or feeling. All the while, I was asking God: "Why am I alive?"

It was a long, arduous journey to find the place where I could finally embrace my authentic self, love myself fully, and find peace with being unique. It's been a battle from which I suffered many scars, but I've never stopped fighting.

I decided to publish the book (with Anton's approval) in hopes that others may find inspiration to live their truth and fully accept themselves, as well.

Anton's Book is the allegorical story of Mark, a young college student who appears to have it "all together". But none of his friends, family, or professors seems to notice that Mark's in the midst of a spiritual crisis. On a holiday trip home, Mark is confronted with a choice that could dramatically alter the course of his life and lead him to the peace he's been seeking. His journey will force him to face his truth and his image.

The book is comprised of three parts. Part 1, "The Search", is a poem about Mark's pursuit of something he's desperate to recover. Part 2, "The Station", is the tale of Mark's mystical journey during his senior year of college. Finally, "The

Satchel" is a selection of life lessons that I hope will be of value to you in your personal journey and encourage you to live with greater purpose, peace, self-acceptance, and authenticity.

-ERIC GARVANNE, JR., 2018

Football Game (2010)

THE SEARCH

Each day when he awoke,
And at night before sleep,
Into the window of glass,
An image he would seek.

Conveyed through his eyes,
A small trace of light,
Struggled to pierce the darkness
To see the other side.

But today was like the others,
Where the pain was too real
To overcome the internal
So his heart would again feel.

So he adjusted his worn mask
To start another day,
Then turned from the mirror
And walked away.

THE STATION

◆

"How many times do I have to tell you that I'm tired? I'm fucking tired of being tired! I didn't ask you for this!" The anger was becoming so intense he could feel his blood cooking. "Are you even listening?"

No response. Typical. As if he expected this time to be different.

"Why am I even here? I just want this to be over!"

Like countless nights before, Mark was battling in his own 'Ground Zero'. His stomach was in knots, his head throbbing with pain. The bedroom was filled with a heavy darkness matched by his internal emptiness. With tears streaming down his face, Mark was finally so exhausted that he collapsed on his bed. "I give up."

Alone, once again, Mark desperately sought a way to escape the pain of being trapped in a situation he didn't understand nor could explain. As he laid back to rest his head on the pillow, feeling helpless and hopeless, he stared intensely at the ceiling's blank white canvas and made a final request of God: "How can I make sure that I don't wake up tomorrow?"

A few hours after falling asleep, his 4:00 a.m. alarm went off. As soon as his eyes opened, his first thought: "Damn! I'm still alive." Disappointed, Mark knew he'd have to endure another day of hiding his pain from the eyes of the world. He rolled out of bed and forced himself to talk to a God he doubted cared enough to even listen. Then he began searching for the mask he thought he left by the mirror the previous night.

Still exhausted and emotionally drained, Mark went outside for his pre-dawn run before heading to campus. With the streetlights guiding his path, he found an inkling of joy as he thought about finishing his winter mid-term exams and traveling home to Norwood for the two-week holiday break. He could at least look forward to getting away from the stress of school, work, and trying to secure a "real" job after graduation that upcoming spring. It was a welcomed break from pondering all his future uncertainties.

Before leaving for campus, Mark grabbed his keys, wallet, backpack, and, most importantly, his mask. Mark took his mask everywhere. He had worn it so much that it had become a subconscious act to put it on every day. He didn't remember how old he was when he started wearing the mask, where it came from, or how he came to desperately depend on it. But Mark felt that his mask was his protection and he feared being seen without it.

As he drove to campus, everything felt heavy — his head, shoulders, legs, even his heart felt as though an anchor was tied to it. His breaths were noticeably short and a cloud was forming around his head. After pulling into a parking spot, he sat for a moment, in silence, observing the scenes playing out on the other side of his windshield. He considered whether it was worth the effort to step out of his car and walk to class or simply return to his apartment.

Similar to every other day, Mark had work to do that morning. He had to endure another day of being the guy with the bright future ahead of him and who had all the answers. But if people really knew what was behind the mask, they'd realize that Mark wasn't they guy they thought he was.

Once making the decision to get out, he started polishing the mask, checking for any exposed cracks that needed to be covered. Having done this for so many years, Mark applied his mask meticulously and methodically, almost mindlessly.

As he walked across campus toward the Economics building for his last mid-term, he tried to limit his interactions with friends—and "associates"—who wanted to talk. But that was a pointless endeavor, because it seemed as though he ran into everyone who wanted to talk that day. But with the skills of a crafty politician, he kept the conversations short, shallow, and directed primarily at the other person.

Mark was good at playing the 'Redirect Game'. He learned early in life that people love to talk about themselves, and it's easy to shift conversations about you back to them without the other person realizing—or even caring—that they've started talking about themselves again. With very few exceptions, this tactic of redirection seemed to work well whenever he struggled to keep his mask on.

◆◆◆

As Mark maneuvered through the crowded terminal with his luggage, he was anxious to get to his train, lean back in his seat, and remove his mask for a while. He was mentally, emotionally, and physically exhausted.

When he approached the train platform, Mark noticed that the number and destination city wasn't posted on the train. He also realized that the train's locomotive hadn't been connected yet. He told himself, "Stop over-analyzing, and just get on the damn train." But he couldn't help himself, as usual. So he approached the conductor, who was standing in the middle of the platform. Handing the conductor his ticket, he asked, "Am I at the right platform for the 5:30 train to Norwood? I don't see the train number listed."

After examining the ticket, the conductor briefly stared at him before responding, "Yes, Mark, this is your train."

"Well, the locomotive isn't connected yet. So is it still leaving on schedule? I have family picking me up in Norwood and need to let them know if I'm going to be late."

"Don't worry, we're on schedule. We just had to bring in a different locomotive to pull this train." The conductor began walking down the platform but he stopped and turned back to face Mark. "You should find your seat and relax while you can. You look exhausted." He paused, briefly, staring at Mark, as if questioning whether he should say more. But then he turned and continued walking down the platform toward the front of the train.

"That was odd," Mark thought. But at least he knew he was where he was supposed to be.

When he made it on the train, he threw his carry-on bag on the rack above his window seat, took out his earbuds, and sat down to finally relax. Several minutes later, he felt the impact of the locomotive making its connection. Then the conductor made an announcement apologizing for the impact of the locomotive and confirming that they would be departing the station in ten minutes, as scheduled. With a jam-packed train, Mark was surprised when the seat next to him remained empty. But he was grateful for the extra leg-room and a trip free of having to make small-talk with someone else.

As he put in his earbuds, he felt that someone was staring at him. He looked up and caught the eyes of a boy—maybe 6 years old—staring back at him from across the aisle, three rows up. The boy was staring as though he knew Mark, but Mark couldn't remember ever seeing this child before. After what seemed to be an uncomfortable length of time, the boy took his eyes off Mark and turned back around in his seat. "Okay, so that was odd."

As the train slowly pulled out of the terminal, the conductor made his way down the aisle to check on the passengers. "So, Mark, how are you? Everything okay, so far?"

"Uh, yeah. Thanks for asking. But how do you know my name?"

"Remember, I saw your ticket before you boarded. Anyway, get yourself some rest. And you might as well put away that mask because it won't help you here."

Suddenly feeling exposed and confronted, Mark immediately returned fire. "Wait! What?

What does that even mean? I'm good. Uh, have we met before or something?"

Ignoring his questions, the conductor continued his walk down the train car. "Get some rest, Mark."

Mark had to catch himself before he went into 'over-analyzing' mode. "It's been a long semester. Let me just sit here and relax." He put his earphones back in, leaned his seat back, and finally closed his eyes. His journey was underway.

"Good evening passengers. This is your conductor speaking. We'll be making our first stop shortly. If this is your stop, thank you for riding with us today, and please make sure you've gathered all of your carry-on items before leaving the train." Mark, coming out of his nap, tuned into the conductor's announcement over the intercom. "If this is not your final destination, I'll be making another announcement in a few minutes with our scheduled departure from this station. Thank you."

Mark, now confused and trying to process what he'd just heard, started looking for the conductor. He spotted him walking down the car aisle. "Excuse me, but I'm supposed to be on the express train to Norwood. Why are we stopping? Didn't you tell me I was boarding the right train back at the terminal?"

"Yes, you're on the right train. But we had to include a few stops along the way. But no worries, you're still on schedule."

Mark looked down to check his watch, but the face of the watch was blank, displaying only a transparent glass cover and metal backing. He immediately reached for his phone, which showed only a black screen—no cell service, time…nothing. He looked up at the conductor, who was still standing in the aisle patiently watching Mark's attempts to make sense of what was happening. Mark suddenly sensed that the train was moving unusually fast to be running on tracks. He turned to the window and saw what he could only conceptualize as numerous fragmentations of vivid cities and countrysides speeding past. Shaken, Mark tried to calm himself with the thought that he was dreaming. "I must still be sleeping. Okay, just relax and try to wake up so you can get back to reality."

Mark leaned his head against the headrest, but just before closing his eyes he noticed that the conductor was saying something to the boy from across the aisle, but Mark couldn't hear what was being said. He looked at the boy, who then locked his eyes on Mark as if he was reading him. "Okay, I'm really tripping. I've got to wake up."

The boy turned back around in his seat, and the conductor turned back to Mark. "This isn't a dream, Mark. No matter how much you sit there trying to convince yourself that you're still asleep, you know it's pointless. You know that if this were simply a dream, you would see yourself in it. But you're not seeing yourself, nor are you seeing any representation yourself. Instead, what you're experiencing is happening as if you're looking out from your own eyes, feeling sensations and emotions that are outside of a dreamlike state. You already know this, and that's what's scaring you right now."

"Who the hell are you?"

"I'm your conductor. I hope you got your rest."

"What?"

"We'll talk again, soon. I need to speak with the train engineer in preparation for our first stop."

After turning to walk down the aisle, the conductor stopped at the boy's seat and knelt to say something. After a brief exchange, the conductor exited through the narrow passageway at the front of the car.

"Maybe it's all a dream within a dream," Mark thought. "Yeah, that makes sense. If I can just close my eyes and get back to sleep, I'll wake up from this episode and everything will be cool."

Mark laid his head back and tried to think of being with his family. But as he looked out his window, he heard himself say, "I'm a long way from Norwood."

As Mark began to open his eyes, he knew something had changed. The train was still moving rapidly, but every seat was empty. He felt the presence of someone approaching, but when he looked around he saw no one, not even the conductor. Yet, the feeling of someone's presence intensified. He looked down at the aisle floor, catching the sight of impressions forming in the carpet, like those of footsteps. Without warning, an intense bright yellow light flashed in front of his face, forcing his head back against the window.

Temporarily blinded, his eyes burned as if exposed to a flame while his body vibrated uncontrollably. His heart was pounding as though desperate to escape his chest. Five minutes, 10 seconds, an hour, a day... Mark had no idea how much time passed before feeling the sensation of a warm hand searing through his chest cavity. Instantly, his body began to calm itself. His breathing eased and his heart rate relaxed. Slowly, his eyes refocused and Mark could see the empty car again. But he knew he wasn't alone. Still unseen, he knew the Presence was now beside him.

An amorphous blue light radiated in the seat next to Mark. With an inaudible voice his rational mind couldn't process, the Presence spoke clearer than any human voice he ever heard. "Hello Mark."

"Who... What are... Where am... ?"

The Presence interjected, "Mark, we have much to do, and time is of the essence. So I need you to stop your rational mind from trying to make sense of what's happening. It will only cause you more trouble in your journey.

"The first stop is approaching. It will serve you well to remove your programmed concept of time and space, because that's not how things work here. And if you make the choice to get off the train at the next stop, you will find that your mask doesn't function as you've become accustomed. But you already know that, don't you?"

Not waiting for a response, the Presence continued, "No, you're not here by accident. You're *where* you're supposed to be, and in the *time* you're supposed to be. When the train pulls into the terminal ahead, you will face your next series of decisions. Every decision will have an impact that's greater than yourself. And you will have to own every decision you make.

"To find the answers you've been seeking, you'll have to look within and discover your power and your truth. But that's a choice only you can make, Mark.

"Trust your spirit—not your eyes, not your ears, not your intellect, not your mask. They will lie to you. But the more you trust your spirit, the clearer its voice will become. You won't understand everything you witness. You will have more questions than answers. You will feel things you can't explain. And you will, at times, feel extremely alone and isolated. But don't try to make sense of everything. Keep moving forward and trust the voice within."

As Mark sat speechless, the amorphous blue light turned into a purple shimmering light. "It's time for me to move. The conductor will return shortly. Listen carefully to him. He's been assigned to you for a reason."

At that moment, another flash of intense light struck Mark. When his eyes re-opened all the passengers where in the car again, as though nothing had happened.

✦✦✦

Mark saw the conductor approaching from the passageway at the front of the car, moving at a faster pace than usual and carrying a brown leather satchel over his right shoulder.

Sitting in the seat next to Mark, the conductor removed the satchel from his shoulder. "It's time."

"Time for what, exactly? I don't understand…"

"There's going to be a lot that you don't understand, Mark, a lot that's not going to make sense. But I'm going to ask that you focus and listen right now. I need for you to be present with me." He handed Mark the satchel. "This is for you."

Mark cautiously removed the straps from the front of the satchel and pulled out a metallic blue box. On top of the box was a circular diagram with his name engraved in red. But he couldn't make out what the diagram was supposed to represent.

"This has been prepared for you. When the time is right, open it. What's inside will help you navigate what's ahead."

"How do I know when that time is?"

"Because it will tell you. You just have to stay attentive and listen for its voice."

"I was told that time and space doesn't work here."

"Wrong. You were told that your *concept* of physical time and space doesn't work here. Time and space here—where you are now—is different than what you've been taught. So, you're going to have to think differently about what you see, hear, and experience. Just like when you looked out that window and tried to make sense of the images you saw passing by, or when you realized that we're not running on tracks, don't limit your understanding to what you think is possible."

"Where am I going? I just wanted to go home. I just wanted to have a normal life. I didn't ask for all of this. I didn't ask to be here!"

"You've spent most of your life trying to convince everyone that you only wanted to live a normal life. You tried to convince yourself that if you could only be who everyone expected you to be, then you'd be happy. You tried to convince the world that you were 'okay'. But you haven't found peace with the mask you use to deflect people from seeing who you truly are. All the while, you're running from what you sincerely desire, the man you want to become.

"You assume it's pointless to continue searching for answers to the questions that have kept you restless and depressed. However, there's something within you, like a fire that you haven't found a way to extinguish yet, that's kept alive the faintest of hopes that there's something more— something that you can't understand but know is bigger than you. And that's why you've never been able to find comfort in your mask. It's like a weight you carry with you, every day. You drag it around wherever you go like a dead body that you have a perpetual fear of losing."

"How do you know this?"

"Look, you'll never have a 'normal' life. So, cancel that idea."

Mark felt the train accelerate faster, but when he turned to the window, he was shocked to see a brightly lit cityscape moving past in slow motion. It completely contradicted the speed at which his body told him the train was moving. It was like a vivid animation displaying itself strictly for him.

Ahead was a skyscraper with a clock tower at its highest point. An ominous sensation suddenly overcame Mark. The clock's face morphed, taking on human facial features. Its eyes opened and looked directly at Mark through the passing train window. Time felt suspended. With a voice that sent chills through Mark's body, the clock's face extended itself from the tower and asked Mark: "Is this the train headed for Norwood?" Something about the voice, and the image, made Mark realize danger was approaching.

The view of the cityscape sped up rapidly, as if catching up with the speed of the train again. As the train entered a tunnel, the lights flickered several times before shutting off. But no one whispered a word. There was a deathly air of silence on the train.

A few moments later, the lights came back on. The train was still moving swiftly through the pitch black tunnel. Mark turned back to the conductor, but the conductor was gone. "Where did he go?" He stood up to look around but the train suddenly decelerated, violently forcing Mark back into his seat. With the train's breaks screeching, his hands clutched the arms of the seat to brace himself for impact. But it never came.

Mark searched to find the little boy from earlier. But he was no longer there. A stranger, whom he had never seen before, was now occupying the boy's seat.

"Good evening, everyone. We are now pulling into our first stop on the way to Norwood. The time is now 5:40 p.m. We will be at the station until…" Mark didn't hear the end of the statement because the intercom started breaking up. The announcement continued, "…then departing promptly for our next stop. If this is not your final destination but you decide to leave the train while we're here, please make sure you're back in your seat by our scheduled departure time. Thank you."

The conductor left the intercom, walking back through the train to prepare to open the car doors. Mark stood up and grabbed the conductor's arm as he walked by. "I didn't hear what time the train is leaving. How long are we going to be here?"

"Until it's time for us to leave."

"Damn, that's not a clear answer!"

"It wasn't meant to be."

"Where's that boy you were talking to earlier? He was sitting in that seat until just now. Where is he?"

"'*Where* is he?' That's the wrong question. You will be better served asking '*Who* is he?'"

"Well, will you at least tell me *who* he is? I've seen you talking to him, so I know you must know something about him."

"Why are you concerned about that boy, Mark?"

Mark immediately felt exposed. His natural instinct told him to reach for his mask. But the conductor stopped him. "Choices, Mark. Your choices will determine whether you find the answers your spirit seeks, the peace you're searching for, the sense of home where you desperately want to arrive.

"Now, you have a set of options. You can choose to stay on the train during this stop and search for the mask you think you've lost, get off the train while we're here and explore what's waiting for you outside, or go to the station terminal and try to find another way to Norwood. It's up to you. But whatever choice you make, you will have to own. And each choice will lead to another set of choices. So the journey goes."

"If I get off the train, where would I go? And when would I need to return so I don't miss the departure?"

"Take the satchel. Stay attentive. Stay on your path. And you'll know when it's time to return. I have to open the doors for the passengers, Mark. We have to stay on schedule. See you soon."

Mark sat for a moment, watching several passengers as they grabbed their carry-on bags and headed for the doors. He also wondered about those who had decided to stay onboard. As he was looking around, Mark caught a glimpse of his mask, which had fallen in the crack between his seats. He looked at his mask. He looked at his satchel. And then Mark made his choice.

Christmas Eve (2009)

Fishing Trip (2018)

THE SATCHEL

➔

AUTHENTICITY

- When you are being you, you are uncopiable. When you are being you, you separate yourself from the noise. When you are being you, you become known as an original.

- Don't dwell on negative thoughts about what others may think of you. Stay authentic, sincere, and mindful of your value.

- You're a walking advertisement; so what message are you advertising to those who experience you?

- *"Today you are You, that is truer than true. There is no one alive who is Youer than You."* ~Dr. Seuss

- To be authentic, you have to be willing to give up everything except your truth.

- Consider *who* you want to be, not *what* you want to be. Ask yourself: "Who is the person I'm striving to become?" And the *what* will take care of itself.

- *"Be the change you want to see in the world."* ~Mahatma Gandhi

- You are different; you don't fit-in with the crowd for a reason. Build confidence in the things that make you unique; embrace what makes you stand out.

- *"Live the way you want to be remembered."* ~Unknown

- Consider how you want to be remembered—what your legacy will be—and seek to live that way, every day.

- Live life to the fullest, because you only get one chance to make the most of life.

- *"If a man does not keep pace with his companions, perhaps it is because he hears a different drummer. Let him step to the music he hears, however measured or far away."* ~Henry David Thoreau

- Live to be the exception.

- Make every room you enter better because you're there.

- When you die, all that will really matter is the truth of who you were while you lived.

- It's better to be a person of substance than a person of style.

- *"Be who you are and say what you feel, because those who mind don't matter and those who matter don't mind."* ~Theodor "Dr. Seuss" Geisel

- Don't be afraid to fly alone; find a path that is your own.

- Pursue that which brings you joy, fulfillment, and a sense of purpose. Don't try to be like anyone else. Don't define yourself by a job, paycheck, or what others may say or think. Stay true to yourself; live your truth.

- Words aren't always necessary. Without saying a word, a light fulfills its purpose by simply being what it's created to be—a light. Follow the light's example; be who you were created to be and you'll shine in this world.

BUSINESS

- Look for what's not already mainstream or accepted. Build your business around the opportunities that others miss or are too afraid to pursue.

- When transacting business, stay mindful of the "business" being run behind the business that's being presented to you. Avoid taking the presentation at face-value.

- Never enter into a business transaction without a clear understanding of the terms of the deal.

- Investors don't put their money behind a business idea, rather they invest in the people leading the idea. Investors want to feel secure in *who*, more so than *what*, they're investing in.

- When you take care of God's business, God will take care of yours.

- Be an *owner* instead of an *employee*; value ownership rights more than a paycheck.

- When negotiating, never reveal to the other side that you have a deadline, because they will use "time pressure" against you.

- In negotiating, the person who has more options has greater power. So create your options before you need to use them.

- Never place someone in leadership who values their salary more than your organization's mission.

- Work for a purpose, not a paycheck.

- Never build an organization based on a person or personality; build on a vision, not an individual.

- Always be willing to walk away from a potential opportunity.

COMMUNICATION

- The more you know, the less you need to talk.

- When speaking, slow down and be mindful of how you pronounce your words. Speak clearly, thoughtfully, and intentionally.

- Be more focused on what someone is saying than your response to what they're saying.

- *"To be interesting, be interested."* ~Dale Carnegie

- Be curious of the world around you; be curious of the lives of others. When communicating, let others feel that you're more interested in them than in yourself by spending more time listening and observing than talking. It will make you a more interesting person.

- People hear what they see. What you do speaks louder than what you say.

- When you don't talk too much, people pay more attention when you do speak.

- More important than what a person says is what they communicate.

- There's a clear distinction between venting and complaining. Venting is verbalizing your frustrations, but complaining is doing nothing to change your frustrations.

- When dealing with conflict, search for the intention behind the other person's words. Go to the balcony—rise above the surface—to get an accurate view of the real issues fueling the conflict.

- *"A smart person knows what to say. A wise person knows whether or not to say it."* ~Unknown

- Sometimes the most powerful voice in the room is the one who speaks the least.

- Say what you mean; speak with integrity.

- Talk less and listen more; be *"quick to listen, slow to speak and slow to become angry"*. ~James 1:19

- It's more powerful to be a great listener and observer than to fill the air with unnecessary words.

- Listening Deeply = Influence.

- The most powerful way to gain influence is unspoken.

- Listening is an act of respect. If people sense that you're sincerely listening and want them to succeed, you will earn their respect.

- Being a good listener opens up a wealth of meaningful relationships and access to information. Listening also reveals your level of sincerity and authenticity.

- Listen with your ears, eyes, heart, and spirit; it will empower you to connect more deeply with people and discern the true message they're communicating.

Discernment

- Never make a decision based on desperation. Whenever you feel pushed into a rushed, uneasy decision, take a step back and think it through. Desperate decisions are always a mistake.

- Trust God more than your emotions.

- Learn how to sit back and observe. You're not required to respond to every situation.

- Emotional intelligence (EQ) is knowing when to be silent and give people enough space to hear their inner voice. It's being self-aware enough to know when your silence is more effective than your advice.

- Trust your judgement, trust your gut. Even when outward appearances, circumstances, or the opinions of others try to convince you that you're wrong, trust what your spirit is telling you.

- The obvious answer isn't always the best one. Look past the obvious in search of a possibly better, hidden solution.

- Times and seasons change. It's important to know what season you're in at any given moment. Discerning the seasons enables you to be more effective in carrying out God's purpose for your life.

- When the crowd is moving in one direction, look in the other. Don't be lulled into blindly following the footsteps of the crowd.

- Don't enlist yourself into every battle that's presented to you. Use your discernment in choosing which battles to engage in and which ones to walk away from.

- Emotional intelligence (EQ) will open more opportunities than academic intelligence.

- Constantly investigate areas in which you can cut the waste from your life—unhealthy relationships, distractions, negativity, etc. The more waste you hold onto, the more toxic your life will become.

- When being advised by people who are mostly saying the same thing, listen carefully to the one or two persons voicing something different, regardless of their position. Their voice may be giving you the best advice you need to hear.

- When you ask something of someone, regardless of what they say, their actions will reveal their honest response. Never trust what someone says when their actions are telling you something different.

- Crafting good questions leads to creative solutions to problems. When facing a problem, start with asking yourself questions about the problem.

- Obedience to God is the compass you need to navigate your journey.

- *"God writes straight with a crooked line."* ~Grandma Isabelle Mullgrav

- Emotions are natural, but it's important to be an *observer* rather than a *reactor* to your emotions. Learn to use your emotions to think; don't let your emotions do the thinking for you.

FAILURE

- A warrior suffers from the pain of defeat. But after all has passed, he still knows that war is made of many battles; and thus he continues on.

- Everyone makes mistakes. However, high achievers recognize the patterns causing their mistakes, and they stop repeating them.

- Sometimes you win by losing. Giving up a current opportunity may be worth the price of receiving a greater future opportunity.

- Don't lose the war for the sake of winning a battle.

- There are times when you must walk away from the battle—and be willing to look as though you've lost—in order to win the war.

- Don't be afraid to fail; remember failure isn't forever.

- Sometimes rejection can point you in the direction of a greater opportunity you didn't know existed. Look for the doors God may be opening as a result of the doors rejection closed.

- If you're going to achieve anything meaningful, you will endure failures. But it's through the failures of experimentation that you achieve success. Though you must be willing to fail in order to succeed, your successes will far outweigh your failures.

- *"I never lose. I either win or learn."* ~Nelson Mandela

- Don't look at mistakes with regrets, but rather as lessons from which to learn.

- It's better to take a risk and fail than to question later in life, "What if ... ?"

- It's better to be yourself and fail than to be an imitation and succeed.

- Some people will use failure as motivation to succeed, while others use it as an excuse to give up.

- Pay attention when God tells you to prepare your soil, even if you don't know how the seeds will be provided or what seeds you should plant. Keep your soil ready, because you never know when planting season may arrive.

- The call of God is always disruptive. It will disrupt the life you've become comfortable with. God's call requires a step of faith into an uncertain future. God will stir things up in your life when he calls, and he will call you to do what you think you can't. However, embrace the disruption, follow where God leads, and know that God's preparing you for something better as a result of the disruption.

- Be content with living in the adventures and unpredictability of God's plan for your life.

- Don't wait for the famine to arrive before you start planting seeds for a harvest.

- Put God first in everything you do; trust that his plan is best.

- When God puts something on your heart to do, just do it.

- Use the tools, talents, and wisdom you already possess to move forward with building your dreams, regardless of how limited they may appear. Build, brick by brick, with what you have and what you believe, without succumbing to the fear of the unknown future. God will turn what you thought was simply two fish and five loaves of bread into the fulfillment of dreams you didn't even know you had. Keep building and believing.

- Fear and Faith can't occupy the same space.

- Not everyone will understand why you do what you do, and they don't need to.

- If God's vision for you seems impossible, remember he's not asking you to do it alone. God simply wants you to have enough faith to step out, in obedience, and believe that he can do the impossible through you.

FEAR

- Sometimes God will wait for you to let go of what you fear losing before he blesses you with what you've been seeking. When you recognize that you have a fear of losing something—or someone—it's a sign you're trying to control the situation instead of trusting God.

- There's a sense of freedom that comes from confronting your fears. If you live in fear, it will control you; but when you confront your fear, it loses its power.

- *"Birds learn to fly by falling. We don't fail by falling; we only fail when we stop taking the leap."* ~Mom (Carla Rodrigues)

- Taking a leap of faith is scary, but the safety of the nest is only temporary. If you stay in the nest too long you will either die there or become prey. So when God pushes you out of the nest, take the leap. Trust that the wings God gave you will lift you up, enabling you to soar to unimaginable heights.

- Don't invest in another person's fears. Maintain your own perspective and faith.

- *"Don't let fear put your dreams to sleep."* ~Stevie Wonder

- You have to be willing to take a risk if you want to be successful. You can't stay on the bench. Read, study, save money, make mistakes, and confront your fears. You can't win if you don't get in the game.

- *"You are confined only by the walls you build yourself."* ~Unknown

- Learn to listen through the fear; don't allow fear to silence what you need to hear.

- God's anointing will put you in places of responsibility for which you have no prior experience—and that can be a scary place to be. However, God will provide you with everything you need to succeed, if you keep him first in all you do.

FOCUS

- If you respond to every dog that barks, you'll get nowhere in life.

- Stay mindful of where your attention is being directed. Every emergency and alarm doesn't require your response.

- When you allow yourself to become visibly angry, all you're doing is giving your opponent the advantage. Rise above the anger and stay focused on your progress.

- Attention is a resource; you own it and you must be wise in how you spend it.

- Focus is power. Wherever your focus goes, energy flows.

- Spend more of your time focused on your future, not your past—more on where you're going than where you've been.

- Whatever controls your attention controls your life. So, ask yourself: "What am I giving attention to? What am I focused on?

What am I talking about? What thoughts and activities am I feeding?" If it's not empowering or creating joy, then redirect your attention. Only you can decide what you allow to direct your life.

- Don't let your ego cloud your focus, because those clouds will turn into storms.

- You can't control people, but you can control your actions, responses, and perspective. Focus on what you can control, not what you can't.

- The secret of improving your future is in the present. If you pay attention to the present, you can improve it. And if you improve the present, your future will be better.

- What you focus on will become your reality, whether it's true or not.

- When someone makes a condescending or negative comment toward you, first consider if it's worthy of a response. If not, simply move on with what's important. It's a waste of your valuable time and energy to dwell on negativity.

- Never allow those things that matter least to interfere with those that matter most.

- A distraction will sometimes appear as an opportunity, but its intention is the same as a setback—to stop you from achieving your goals.

- Pay more attention to the process than the profit.

- With so many voices vying for your attention, you must develop the skill of "selective listening". If a voice isn't helping you move toward your goals, exercise caution in how much attention you offer it.

GRATITUDE

- Happiness is not a destination. Be grateful along the journey; make the most of it. Discover the joy, meaning, and purpose within the journey.

- When you have gratitude in your heart, it permeates throughout your entire being and impacts those who experience your presence.

- Living in a state of gratitude impacts what's attracted to you.

- Somewhere in the world there's someone dreaming they had the life you have right now. So live with gratitude for what you already have instead of complaining about what you don't.

GROWTH

- Strive for growth, not comfort, because the world, people, and circumstances are constantly changing. Nothing stays the same.

- Never become intoxicated with comfort.

- Be a river, not a swamp. Swamps simply pool water, with nothing new coming in or old moving out. But rivers keep their waters flowing, gradually forging new paths.

- Study what you desire to become.

- Never stop asking questions. Never assume you have all the answers. Be a researcher of life, not an expert.

- Sometimes God will remove your options and push you to make the changes necessary to enter a new phase of life.

- When God says it's time to let something (or someone) go, let it go and trust that he has better in store for you. In order to grow, you have to learn to let go.

- You must continue studying, learning, and sharpening your tools. Don't be discouraged when things aren't moving as fast as you had hoped. Originality takes time to develop; it can't be rushed.

- *"Being realistic is the most commonly traveled road to mediocrity."* ~Will Smith

- Growth requires discomfort. To achieve what others don't, you have to do what others won't. Everyone experiences discomfort and the fear of change. But what separates the successful is that they're willing to fight through the discomfort, while the ordinary remain comfortable in their mediocrity.

INTEGRITY

- Trying to force someone to respect you only makes them respect you less. Respect isn't bought, forced, or given; it's earned.

- It's not enough simply stand against the status quo; your life and work must convey that you stand *for* something. It's in standing for something, with integrity, that you earn respect and the willingness of others to follow your leadership.

- Be honest and upfront with people, especially with those you lead. Don't exaggerate, because every exaggeration of the truth, once detected, destroys your credibility. When you exaggerate, you'll lose the respect of others, and it will be assumed your words can't be trusted.

- People work better and harder for leaders they trust.

- It's more convincing when someone talks positively about you than when you talk about yourself.

- God is much more concerned with your character than your comfort.

- More important than what you do is how you do it. Live, work, and play with integrity.

- Respect isn't dependent on fame, money, or power. So don't become a man who chases after them to gain—or maintain—the respect of others.

- Don't bend to social pressures that require you to compromise your integrity. Be willing to embrace the isolation, solitude, and suffering necessary to build something truly great.

- Never allow the fear of being hurt to cause you to be inconsistent in your character.

LEADERSHIP

- A manager desires a title, while a leader seeks none.

- Lead through influence, not a title.

- *"A mediocre teacher tells. A good teacher explains. A superior teacher demonstrates. A great teacher inspires."* ~William Arthur Ward

- People who inspire typically don't pursue notoriety or acknowledgement for what they do; they're not concerned with who gets the credit.

- Strive not to simply play the game, but to change the way the game is played.

- When someone is placed in a high-pressure situation, most often, their natural tendencies will be on display. It's difficult for a person to cover-up who they truly are in those moments, and it provides a good window to view who that person is beneath the surface.

- A key element of your success will be the success of those you lead.

- *"A king doesn't have to wear a crown for his subjects to know he's the king."* ~Unknown

- A manager serves himself, while a leader serves the people. A manager seeks to promote himself, while a leader seeks to promote others. A manager directs, while a leader guides. A manager says, "Go!", while a leader says, "Let's Go!"

- A leader never tells those he leads to do something he isn't willing to do himself.

- You have to lead yourself before you can truly lead someone else.

- The true test of leadership isn't shown when facing issues under your control, but rather when forced to confront situations you can't control. You can prepare and create great plans for what you think is coming, but real leadership is being

---

prepared for the unexpected crisis that may arise at any moment.

- As a leader, don't allow fear, influence, or a desire for acceptance to make you compromise what God's directing you to do. A leader has to be led by a higher purpose rather than a need to appease others.

- Innovative leaders never stop learning. They seek to learn from people and experiences, from successes and failures. They possess an ability to be taught by those with whom they come in contact, and they aren't threatened by intelligent people from whom they can learn. Further, they expect and encourage this behavior from the people they lead. This attitude fosters innovation and growth throughout their command.

- A leader needs to know when to step aside and allow those he's led to step-up and take the lead.

- As a leader, you have to be okay with being uncomfortable and making unpopular decisions.

- Leadership requires patience, perseverance, and a willingness to be misunderstood.

- When disaster or disorder strikes, be the eye of the storm. As a leader, be the center of calm confidence and self-assurance. People turn to the leader to determine how they should respond. So maintaining a presence of calm confidence increases your performance, as well as the performance of those you lead.

- There are two kinds of leaders: one who enters a room and says: "Here I am", and the other who enters a room and the people say: "There he is". When you're a genuine leader, you don't have to announce yourself as one; people recognize and announce it for you.

- A leader doesn't bestow the title of "leader" upon himself; it's a designation given him by those who choose to follow.

- In a crisis, if you wait until you know everything and have all the information, you'll be too late. Sometimes you must make decisions based on very limited knowledge. You will have to take calculated risks to lead effectively and earn the respect of your team.

- If you have to remind people you're the leader, you're not the leader.

- *"I would say that [a master] is not someone who teaches something, but someone who inspires the student to do his best to discover a knowledge he already has in his soul."* ~The character Tetsuya in Paulo Coelho's *The Way of the Bow*

- A leader lives with the knowledge that others will never fully understand all he endured to build the road that makes their journey a little easier to travel.

OPPORTUNITY

- Stay aware of what's going on around you. Often, the most extraordinary opportunities are hidden among seemingly insignificant events.

- Opportunity is often found in uncomfortable places; but if you spend your time complaining and focusing on the negative you won't recognize the opportunity God's scheduled to meet you in those places. Remember, the discomfort is only temporary.

- When you start taking steps toward your dreams, you'll be amazed at the unexpected doors of opportunity that will open in your life. So, just start moving.

- Be honest with yourself when deciding which opportunities to pursue. Avoid committing to anything that will take you off your path.

- Big challenges always precede major blessings.

- It's more important to be present than productive. Being present creates meaningful productivity, along with deeper insights and less anxiety.

- God will bring you to a place of discomfort and pain to push you to release the baggage that's holding you back from experiencing new opportunities.

- Sometimes you have to close one door before the next one will open.

- Always prepare for the opportunities that have yet to present themselves.

- Whatever you want to do in life, prepare for it now, so when the opportunity comes you'll be ready to take action.

PATIENCE

- A patient person is always richer than an impatient one because the patient can always afford to wait. The patient person is never desperate.

- Patience enables you to see the big picture; it helps you make the most of today, while building for a better tomorrow.

- Don't let your deadlines interfere with God's timing.

- Trust God's timing in all things, regardless of outside pressures.

- Sometimes God's delay in answering a prayer is actually him protecting you from something you haven't seen. So remain patient and faithful with God's process.

- If you put the cart before the horse, the horse will run it over every time. You can't rush success.

- Remember that your current situation is not indicative of your future success.

- Don't argue with people about the timeline God has you on. God has a pace that's set specifically for you.

- Peace is more valuable than money, so never allow money to make your decisions. Always follow the path of peace.

- Don't kill your future based on your past.

- *"Fools give full vent to their rage, but the wise bring calm in the end."* ~Proverbs 29:11

- Control your emotions; don't let them control you. Preserve your peace before others, regardless of what's going on around you. Maintain an inner-circle of trusted people who will help you regulate your public displays of emotions.

- Don't give people permission to steal your peace.

- Don't return to something God's removed from your life. There's no value in trying to reclaim what God's already freed you from. Live forward.

- A key to strengthening your self-confidence and inner peace is to be more concerned with what you think about yourself than what others think about you.

- *"If you are depressed, you are living in the past. If you are anxious, you are living in the future. If you are at peace, you are living in the present."* ~Lao Tzu

- Allow the past to teach you but not possess you.

- Be present; appreciate the moment you're in. Living in the past is unproductive, and worrying about the future is equally unproductive. Take time to reflect on the past and envision your future, but don't settle in either place. Live in the present, the place where you'll find peace.

- You must free yourself from your past in order to live freely in your present.

- Eagles don't fight with chickens. If you want to soar with eagles, you can't spend your time fighting in the chicken coop.

- *"Stop planting flowers in people's yards who aren't going to water them."* ~Unknown

- Invest in relationships with people who value building a relationship with you. Don't stay in relationships where you're taken for granted or undervalued; shake the dust off your feet and move on.

- If you're normally the smartest person in the room, you need to move to another room. Surround yourself with people wiser than you.

- Invest in those who choose to invest themselves in your leadership and vision.

- Living with unforgiveness is living in a past that you can never change. Accept that what happened in the past, happened. Find healing for yourself and move on.

- There are two types of friends in life: Growth Friends and Maintenance Friends. The first group are friends you grow with, while the second are ones content with simply being connected to you. It's important you know the difference.

- Success is a journey, not a destination. Surround yourself with people who push you to be better today than you were yesterday.

- Allow the time and space for new relationships to grow. Don't try to rush a relationship in hopes of turning it into something you think you want. Give people enough space to demonstrate whether they value having you as a friend, business partner, etc.

- An important factor in remaining focused and grounded is to invest in relationships with focused, grounded people. Invest in relationships that make you better, that add value to your life.

- Your relationships will become more authentic when you focus on being "present" for others.

- *"It takes a long time to grow an old friend."* ~Unknown

- The pain someone has caused will never go away until you forgive them. That doesn't mean you have to like them, invite them back into your life, or reach out to them. It simply means forgiving them so you can release the negativity and open yourself up to more meaningful relationships and opportunities.

- Some things from the past need to stay there. Avoid reconnecting with people and situations from the past that have no meaningful purpose in your present or future.

- Maintain a presence that makes people want to be better when they're around you.

- Never allow selfish pride or ego to be the cause of losing a friend.

- In the equation of life, people are either adding or subtracting value from you. In order to grow, remove the negative variables from your equation.

- You're not responsible for another person's happiness. You can help influence it, but it's not your job to make someone feel happy. A person has to decide for himself whether to be happy. That's why it's important to establish the proper boundaries in your relationships.

- *"The key is to keep company only with people who uplift you, whose presence calls forth your best."* ~Epictetus

- Surround yourself with people who inspire you.

- Never accommodate people who refuse to help themselves, because by accommodating them you become their enabler.

- A friendship that hasn't been tested is a friendship that can't be trusted.

- Never settle for the ordinary when greater is meant for you.

- If you don't make plans of your own, you'll become a cog in the wheel of someone else. They will determine your direction, limitations, and time value. You will work to make their vision a reality at the expense of your own.

- It's not enough to believe in yourself; you also have to put your belief into action. Your self-belief has to be demonstrated in order for it to have any meaning.

- Walk purposely. Walk fearlessly. Walk intentionally.

- Each day, ask yourself: "Is what I'm doing today getting me closer to where I want to be tomorrow?" Are you doing the work, performing the disciplines, and making the decisions necessary to move closer to your goals?

- If you sit in a negative environment long enough, you will eventually convince yourself that it's normal. In order to get out of that environment, you must be willing to stand up and make a move for yourself.

- When people say that your goal is impossible, remember that their statement is an opinion, not a fact. Don't allow people's opinions to become your facts.

- Do the work, instead of wasting time talking about the work.

- Life's too short to wait around for people to give you their approval or validate your goals. If there's something you believe you're meant to do, then go for it. Regardless of what happens, at least you can respond to your critics: "I tried. What about you?"

- Like an ant, never quit looking for a way to get where you're supposed to be. If ants are headed somewhere and you try to stop them, they'll look for another way. They'll climb over, under, and around you. They will constantly seek another way. Ants will gather all they can in the summer to prepare for winter. They don't have quotas or "good enough" philosophies. They don't gather a certain amount and then head back to the mound to hang out. If the ant can do more, it does.

- Sometimes you have to make yourself uncomfortable and remove the safety nets in order to live the life you want. Being uncomfortable pushes you to strive for more. It's better to live a life pursuing what you truly desire than to be complacent and miserable by simply existing through life.

- You will never find a strong person who had an easy past.

- When days seem dark and difficult, look ahead and know that one day the pain and sacrifice will be worth the success.

- A boy chases; a man hunts. Be a man.

- It's the small disciplines that lead to great accomplishments.

- Without self-discipline, focus, and hard work, talent will get you nowhere.

- Progress, not perfection; measure each day by the progress you make, not perfection.

- Talent, by itself, will not produce elite performance. To be a champion, training and focus must serve as a complement to your God-given talents.

- Without self-discipline, a dream will never be successful.

- Anything worth achieving will always have roadblocks and setbacks along the way. But you must maintain the fortitude, self-control, and self-discipline to overcome them if you want to attain your dreams.

- Love yourself; don't base your joy or happiness on the actions of others.

- The truest way to differentiate yourself is to fully accept yourself.

- Love yourself first, because you're going to spend the rest of your life with you.

- The most powerful person you can ever be is yourself.

- As long as you consider yourself to be a victim, you'll be dependent upon someone else for your freedom.

- *"Believe in yourself so strongly that the world can't help but believe in you, too."* ~Unknown

- Don't believe everything that's said about you, regardless of the authority of the person saying it.

- The source of high self-esteem is internal; it doesn't need external validation to thrive or crumble at the first sign of a threat. A confident person doesn't need to one-up anyone else.

- Be confident, not arrogant. Arrogance comes from feeling small and insecure inside, while confidence comes from believing in yourself.

- Your words are a blueprint for the life you're creating. Train your words to speak what you desire to become; avoid negative self-talk. Speak life to, and about, yourself.

- To refrain from anger when being unjustly criticized or attacked is a sign of self-confidence.

- *"When you learn how much you're worth, you'll stop giving people discounts."* ~Unknown

- If you have something no one else has, why would you discount it? If you're an original, why would you discount yourself?

- If the grass looks greener on the other side of the fence, maybe it's because there's a leaking septic tank over there. Instead of envying what you assume someone else has, focus on watering your own yard.

- Self-pity is counterproductive. If you resist it, you'll place yourself in a better position in life than most.

- When you're going for your dreams there will be times when you will appear odd, foolish, and unpopular. You won't always look cool and classy. It takes courage to go against the grain of what the crowd thinks you should do.

- *"Don't compare yourself to others. Compare yourself to the person you were yesterday."* ~Unknown

- Don't fear rejection. Rejection is a power you choose to give someone. Nobody can reject you without your permission. The only opinion about you that matters is your own.

- You will never value anything you don't understand. If you want to value yourself, you must first understand yourself.

Success

- Success is a meaningless journey, if you don't have someone to take it with you.

- Every day, make time to plan, execute your plan, evaluate your plan, and adjust your plan.

- *"Work hard in silence. Let your success make the noise."* ~Unknown

- When it comes to success, don't wait for something to happen *to* you; make something happen *for* you.

- Successful people have a simplicity of both purpose and plan. They're hyper-focused on a specific objective and a clearly defined purpose. Their purpose can be stated in a single, easy-to-understand sentence. Also, they don't have highly-detailed, highly elaborate plans. They focus on the simple activities that will be most effective to achieving their personal and professional goals.

- *"If you want to make the team, go to the gym. If you want to own the team, go to the library."* ~Chris Gardner

- Success is not a destination; it's what you discover along the journey *to* the destination.

- If you want to be successful, you can't do what everyone else is doing.

- Define your success based on the man you desire to be, not the things you desire to possess. When a person defines success and greatness based on money, popularity, status, or material things, he will chase them in hopes of possessing them, thereby defining himself by something that won't last. He will become its slave, because anything a man chases will eventually become his master.

- Success is a lifestyle, a series of actions that shape your life.

- Your future is determined by the choices you make today, not tomorrow.

- Never get comfortable living off your prior success. Be willing to let go of what made you successful in the past so you can embrace what will enable your future success.

- It's a better use of time to build a reputation than a resume. Resumes are irrelevant to most highly successful people. So build a good reputation and do the work.

- *"Don't just aspire to make a living, aspire to make a difference."* ~Denzel Washington

- If you add value to the lives of others, you will always be provided for.

THOUGHTS

- The biggest fight is the one in your mind. Stop trying to fight what other people think about you, because what matters is what you think about yourself.

- *"A man is a product of his thoughts. What he thinks, he becomes."* ~Mahatma Gandhi

- Success on the outside begins with success on the inside. Change your thoughts and you'll change your life.

- *"A bad attitude is like a flat tire. Until you change it, you're not going anywhere."* ~Denzel Washington

- What you believe about yourself will become your vision statement. Protect the messages you validate as truth and what you rehearse in your mind. Ask yourself: "What messages do I believe about myself? What messages am I rehearsing? What am I saying to myself?"

- What you think, you will become.

- Your only limitations are the ones you establish in your mind.

- The words *"I can't"* stops the brain from entering a state of creative problem solving, but *"How can I?"* does the opposite. One phrase stops all dialogue, while the other encourages it. Erase *"I can't"* from your vocabulary.

- The subconscious mind interprets what it hears very literally. The words you speak become your reality. Wherever your words lead, your mind, body and environment will follow. Therefore be extremely deliberate about speaking in ways that are positive and empowering. Speak the life you want to live.

- The quality of your life depends on the quality of your thoughts. Thoughts are like seeds in your minds; whatever you plant and feed will grow.

- If you don't make a conscious effort to decide what to allow into your mind each day, life will simply happen *to* you instead of *for* you.

- You are what you think you are. Your reality is what you decide it to be.

- *"For my thoughts are not your thoughts, neither are your ways my ways," declares the Lord. "As the heavens are higher than the earth, so are my ways higher than your ways and my thoughts than your thoughts." ~Isaiah 55:8-9*

- Don't limit God, because he may have a much bigger—and different—plan than what you think.

- In a world filled with increasing distractions competing for your attention, it's vital to train your mind to seek and embrace periods of rest. In rest, creativity and gratitude flourish.

- Whenever negative thoughts or feelings arise, deconstruct them until they no longer have power to influence you.

- The quality of your thoughts will determine the quality of your life. How you think, you will live.

- The wolf you feed will grow, so make sure you're feeding the right wolf.

- When a person becomes clear about what they actually want in life, their value of time increases.

- If you're going to lose something, lose money, not time. Money is replaceable.

- *"Take time, before Time takes you."* ~Unknown

- Busy people are neither creative nor innovative; they simply do a lot of work. Creativity requires prioritizing personal time for reflection and discovery, not simply looking busy.

- Don't be held captive by the past. If you live in the past, you will miss what the future holds; you'll be so blinded by what *could have been* that you won't see what *can be*.

- Don't spend so much time thinking about your next achievement that you fail to appreciate the time in-between.

- *"Reality has a way of catching up with you."* ~President Barack Obama

- Regularly evaluate where, and with whom, you're spending time. Be discerning of the people you associate with, because they have a strong influence on your philosophy, attitude, perspective, and success.

- How you spend your time can be the difference between dreaming about the life you want and actually living it.

- Treat sleep as one of the most important things you'll do all day. Sleep is important for increasing your emotional intelligence (EQ), managing stress-levels, repairing and recharging your mind and body, and thinking clearly, among other things. Getting a sufficient amount of quality sleep is more important than the quantity of tasks you can accomplish by depriving yourself of sleep.

- Live so that you're not afraid to die; give life everything you have. Pursue the purpose for which God created you. Learn to make the most of meaningful moments.

So whenever death comes, you will die having no regrets.

◆ The most valuable time you have is the present; it's a gift, so don't waste it.

VISION

- *"A lot of times, if you're reaching for the stars, nobody can see what you're seeing, except for the few people who are looking up with you, because everybody else is too busy looking down or around."* ~Kenneth (KT) Leonard

- Many people won't understand why you chose to do the things you do, and that's okay. Keep reaching for your stars.

- Dream bigger than what seems possible. If you can rationally conceive how to make your dream a reality, the dream is too small.

- Believe in your vision, even when nobody else does. See your vision as a reality, even when people respond with doubt. Speak of your vision as being inevitable, even when others respond as if it's impossible.

- It doesn't matter if your vision makes sense or sounds possible. What matters is that *you* believe it's possible and take action to create it.

- You receive what you speak. You can't talk death and reap life. You can't speak negatively and receive positive results. Speak of the vision you see from the mountaintop, not the valley.

- Don't put limits on your vision, because you will never go further, nor reach higher, than your vision. Dream the impossible, and work to make it a reality.

- Sometimes you have to look at your dream from a different angle.

- *"Vision without action is a dream. Action without vision is a nightmare."* ~Japanese Proverb

- The vision serves as the compass to reach your destination, while action is what propels you there.

- Peace comes from living your vision, not the vision someone established for you.

- Have a mission that inspires you every day of your life.

- You will either give attention to your dream or your nightmare; one of the two will consume your energy and time.

WEALTH

- True wealth won't be found on a bank statement.

- Accumulate *moments* rather than *things*.

- If you can't find joy when you have little, you won't find it with much.

- The more you shift your thinking away from working for a paycheck, the more opportunities you'll discover to make money work *for you* rather than you working *for it*.

- Money is a game. Learn how to play the game and compete at the highest levels. As with sports, you need to understand the rules, the language, your opponents, and what you're playing for. However, maintain a healthy perspective while competing. Remember that money is a tool, not a god.

- *"Money can't talk, yet it can make lies look true."* ~South African Proverb

- True wealth creates freedom and wears no disguise, so avoid anything that calls itself "wealth" but results in bondage. Though it may seem appealing at first, it will eventually strangle you.

- You don't have to have money to make money; it takes the *knowledge* of money to make money.

- Self-worth is more important than net-worth.

- Wealth is it not a state of money; it's a state of being. You can have a lot of money and still be poor.

- Poverty is a state of mind, not a state of being. Poverty is about thoughts, not money. What you think, you will create. If you change how you think, you'll change how you live.

- Pursue growth, not greed.

- It's more important to leave a legacy of value rather than money.

- Money without purpose will never fulfill you.

- If money makes your decisions, you'll never stop chasing it; money will be your master and you'll be its slave.

- Without wisdom you will never recognize wealth.

- The wealthy may possess riches, but they are never possessed *by* riches.

- Don't allow the fear of a lack of resources to stop you from creating meaningful experiences with the people you love. Trust God to provide, and he will.

YOUR 'WHY'

- Knowing *why* you're pursuing something is more important than knowing *what* you're pursuing or *how* you're going to pursue it. When you understand the *why*, the *what* and *how* will fall into place.

- Those who lead start with the 'Why'. They recognize that the mission isn't about them; it's about the 'Why'.

- People don't buy *what* you do; they buy *why* you do it.

- *"The person who knows* how *will always work for the person who knows* why." ~Unknown

- Are you reactive or intentional? Are spending your life reacting to what's thrown at you, or are you intentional about making decisions for the life you want to create? If you're not intentional, you're simply reacting to life. When you know and take ownership of your 'Why', you will live intentionally.

■ When your *why* is strong enough, the *how* will reveal itself.

Made in the USA
Middletown, DE
26 October 2023

41450011R00066